A Running Press® Miniature Edition™

Printed in China

9 8 7 6 5 4 3 2
Digit on the right indicates the number of this printing

Library of Congress Control Number: 2012938856

ISBN 978-0-7624-4756-5

Running Press Book Publishers
A Member of the Perseus Books Group
2300 Chestnut Street
Philadelphia, PA 19103-4371

Visit us on the web!
www.runningpress.com

William Shakespeare

by Joelle Herr

RUNNING PRESS
PHILADELPHIA • LONDON

Contents

PART II: TRAGEDIES 104

PART III: COMEDIES 188

Introduction

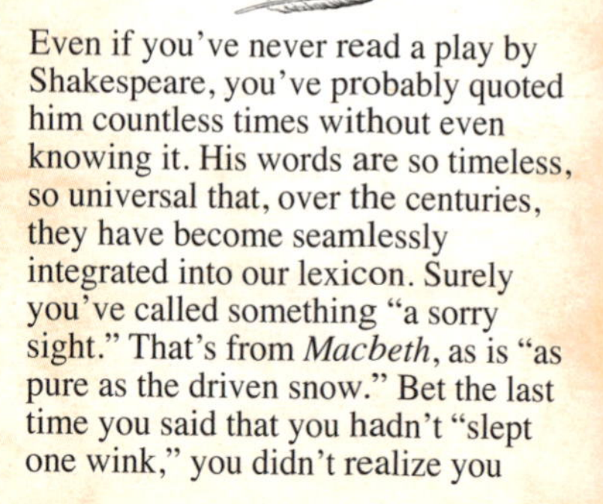

Even if you've never read a play by Shakespeare, you've probably quoted him countless times without even knowing it. His words are so timeless, so universal that, over the centuries, they have become seamlessly integrated into our lexicon. Surely you've called something "a sorry sight." That's from *Macbeth*, as is "as pure as the driven snow." Bet the last time you said that you hadn't "slept one wink," you didn't realize you were quoting *Cymbeline*. Ever been "in a pickle"? Well, so was Trinculo in *The Tempest*. And a "wild goose chase"? That one's from *Romeo and Juliet*.

It's entirely possible that the mere mention of the word Shakespeare makes your eyes glaze over, inducing not-so-pleasant high school flashbacks about tests and stuff. If so, fasten your seatbelt because his plays are actually packed with action galore! Wars, murder, love at first sight, deceit, beheadings, fairies, duels, divorce, marriage, feasts, plays within plays, and, yes, even some "beast with two backs" (*Othello*) action.

Of course it would take you "forever and a day" (*Taming of the Shrew*) to read all of Shakespeare's plays. That's where this book comes in handy—whether you want to get acquainted with the plays in a hurry or are in search of a refresher course. Don't let its diminutive size deceive you, though. In this compact tome, you'll find summaries of all 38 of Shakespeare's plays, along with succinct descriptions of major characters, illustrations, opening lines, and some more iconic lines—efficiently organized for either digesting small chunks at a time or devouring the entirety "at one fell swoop" (*Macbeth*). After all, you can never have "too much of a good thing" (*As You Like It*).

THE Life OF William Shakespeare

In 1623, dramatist Ben Jonson said of Shakespeare: "He was not of an age, but for all time." Boy was that a keen and prescient observation, but perhaps even Jonson would be surprised by just how widely read Shakespeare's plays are more than 400 years after they were written.

We actually don't know too much

about William Shakespeare's life, aside from information found in public records. The son of John Shakespeare, a tradesman, and Mary (Arden) Shakespeare, William was baptized in Stratford, England, on April 26, 1564.

At 18, Shakespeare married Anne Hathaway, who was 26 and already pregnant with their first child. Daughter Susanna was born in May of 1583. Twins Hamnet and Judith followed less than two years later. They had no more children, due to the fact that Shakespeare soon after moved to London, leaving his family behind in Stratford—though still taking care of them financially.

By 1592, Shakespeare was already a rising star—as an actor and playwright—in London's bustling theater scene. The center of this scene was a playhouse called the Theatre, which was succeeded by the Globe, which later opened in 1899. Shakespeare is known to have had an ownership stake in a company called Lord Chamberlain's Men from 1594 to 1603 (the death of Queen Elizabeth I), after which it was called the King's Men (in honor of King James I).

Shakespeare died in April of 1616—some say on his birthday—and is buried in the Holy Trinity Church in Stratford.

With his personal life somewhat mysterious, some have theorized that perhaps Shakespeare's plays were actually written by a group of men or someone else entirely. Though these notions can be neither definitely confirmed nor denied, they are dismissed by most as mere conspiracy theories.

Enough background. It's "high time" (*Comedy of Errors*) we get to the good stuff—the plays.

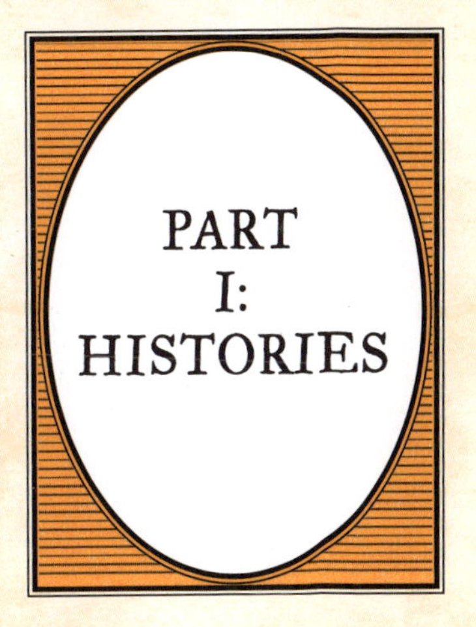

PART I: HISTORIES

Henry IV, Part 1

KING HENRY IV:

So shaken as we are,
so wan with care,
Find we a time
for frighted peace to pant,
And breathe short-winded accents
of new broils
To be commenced
in strands afar remote.

❦ MAJOR ❦ CHARACTERS

Henry IV: His conscience weighs heavily with the guilt of how he came to the throne.

Prince Hal: A rebel prince who goofs off and hangs around with degenerates; a disappointment to his father.

John Falstaff: Old, fat, untrustworthy, and a thief, his wit and lust for life amuse Prince Hal.

Hotspur: Hot-tempered and impulsive, he is the son of the Earl of Northumberland and a foil to Prince Hal.

THE STORY

The play opens with King Henry IV wishing to go on a crusade to the Holy Land but unable to because of unrest and rebellion in his kingdom. Henry is annoyed because his own supporter, Hotspur—son of the Earl of Northumberland, Henry Percy—is refusing to turn over Scottish rebels caught during the recent Battle of Holmedon. Hotspur wishes Henry would pay the ransom for Edmund Mortimer (his brother-in-law), who has been captured by Welshman Owen Glendower. After all, the Percys were instrumental in getting Henry the crown (from Richard II, see page 93), so he kind of owes them a favor. The king refuses Hotspur's request, causing the Percys to decide to band with the Welsh and Scottish rebels in their quest to dethrone Henry.

Meanwhile, the king's son, Prince Hal, has been doing a little rebelling of his own, hanging out with a very *unroyal* crowd of drunks, thieves, and one Sir John Falstaff, who is an old and overweight thief and liar who nonetheless is witty and lives life to the fullest. Falstaff amuses Prince Hal, but Hal realizes that one day he will need to change his ways, step up to the royal plate, as it were, and start acting more princely. This time comes sooner rather than later with Hal receiving instruction from his father to return to the palace because a civil war is imminent. Given a position of high command, Hal promises the king that he will change and claims he will defeat Hotspur in battle to prove his sincerity. Hal asks Falstaff to assemble his own soldiers (who are also unfit for battle, naturally) and join him in the fight.

The Battle of Shrewsbury ensues—without Northumberland, who has fallen ill. Prince Hal saves his father from the sword of the Earl of Douglas, who then moves in to attack

Falstaff, who falls and plays dead. Prince Hal fights and kills Hotspur. Falstaff "miraculously" awakens from his pretend death and sees Hotspur's lifeless body. He impales Hotspur with his sword and loudly claims credit for killing the young Percy—which Hal does not contest.

Henry IV is victorious. He orders the execution of Thomas Percy—and much of the Percy family—but decides to show mercy on Douglas, releasing him. The battle is over, but the war continues, as there are still many who wish to see the king dethroned, including Glendower and Hotspur's father, the Earl of Northumberland.

ICONIC LINE

The better part of valour is discretion.
—Falstaff

Henry IV, Part 2

RUMOUR:

Open your ears;
for which of you will stop
The vent of hearing
when loud Rumour speaks?

❦ MAJOR ❦ CHARACTERS

Henry IV, Prince Hal, and Falstaff **(see page 20)**

Prince John: Shrewd younger brother of Prince Hal.

The Lord Chief Justice: The most powerful man of law in England and a close advisor to Henry IV.

Earl of Northumberland: A rebellious nobleman who keeps withdrawing his support at the last minute before battles — at Shrewsbury this resulted in the death of his son, Hotspur (see page 24).

❧ THE STORY ☙

The play begins where Part 1 left off (see page 25), with England embroiled in civil war. Henry IV has just won the Battle of Shrewsbury, but there are still many rebels—including the Archbishop of York, Thomas Mowbray, and Hotspur's father, the Earl of Northumberland—who want Henry dethroned. Worn down and worn out, the king has become very ill. Prince Hal is feeling guilty for causing his father so much stress with his goofing off.

Falstaff—still taking credit for Hotspur's death—has been promoted to captain, but is as pompous and deceitful as ever. Wanting to keep Prince Hal from associating with Falstaff, Henry IV sends Falstaff away to join his younger son, Prince John, to fight the rebellious forces of Northumberland and York. Falstaff gets himself in and out of various (and amusing) predicaments along the way, stopping in taverns and brothels to recruit men to lead into battle in support of the king.

Northumberland backs out of his commitment to the rebellion—again!—leaving the men of York, Mowbray, and Hastings outnumbered by the king's troops. Word arrives at the rebel camp in Yorkshire that Prince John's troops are closing in and that the prince has been authorized by the king to broker peace with the rebels. John agrees to let the rebels go free and tells them to dismiss their troops. Once the troops have dispersed, though, John goes back on his word and has the rebels arrested and executed.

After hearing the news that the rebellion has been put down, the king takes a turn for the worse. Prince Hal comes to his father's side, and, thinking him dead, takes his crown off his head. The king awakens, aghast, and expresses his disappointment in his son. The prince starts weeping and apologizing and making promises to his father, who forgives him before dying.

Prince Hal is crowned Henry V and assures his brothers and followers that he has put the folly of his youth behind him and will be a strong and just leader. Word of the king's death reaches Falstaff, who is overjoyed with the presumption that great wealth and power will be awarded to him now that his BFF Hal has become the new king. Quite the opposite occurs, though, with the king banishing Falstaff and his cohorts, who are not allowed to be within 10 miles of the king. Henry does offer them an income, though, to keep them from reverting to their old criminal ways.

The king leaves to consult parliament on the stirrings of a war with France.

Henry V

CHORUS:

O for a Muse of fire,
that would ascend
The brightest heaven of invention,
A kingdom for a stage,
princes to act
And monarchs to behold
the swelling scene!

❦ MAJOR ❦ CHARACTERS

Henry V: Recently crowned, he's resolved and an effective orator.

King of France: Rational leader not without a healthy sense of humor.

Bardolph: Henry's friend from his days of carousing; he hasn't changed his ways.

Catherine: Charming and beautiful daughter of the French king—integral to the peace negotiations.

THE STORY

The play opens with the young Henry V ruling over an England that is weary and dispirited after years of civil wars. Plus, Henry's credibility as a leader is hurting from his troubled youth, which was spent carousing with drunkards and criminals—including the infamous Falstaff.

Urged on by the Archbishops of Canterbury and Ely, Henry claims that France belongs to England, which is pretty much a straight-on declaration of war. Sure enough, the French king scoffs at such a suggestion and sends a box of tennis balls to Henry in response. Of course, Henry starts planning his attack on France. Word reaches Henry's old carousing partners and veterans of the recent civil wars—Bardolph, Pistol, and Nim—who prepare to join the troops heading to France. Before they leave, they lament the recent death of Falstaff.

On his way to France, Henry discovers an assassination plot—instigated by the French king—involving three of his noblemen, whom he orders to be executed. Once in France, Henry and his troops are victorious in several battles. Bardolph is sentenced to death by hanging for looting. On the night before the Battle of Agincourt, Henry disguises himself as a commoner and mingles with his soldiers, trying to raise their spirits. The English win the battle—despite being outnumbered five to one—and the French surrender.

In the negotiations for peace, Henry agrees to let the French king stay on the throne, but in return, Henry asks to marry the French king's daughter, Catherine. Henry speaks no French, and Catherine no English, so their first meeting is interesting, to say the least. As part of the peace treaty, their son will inherit the crowns of both England and France. The play ends with the celebration surrounding the birth of the future Henry VI (see page 44).

ICONIC LINE

We few, we happy few,
we band of brother;
For he to-day
that sheds his blood with me
Shall be my brother.
—Henry V

Henry VI, Part 1

BEDFORD:

Hung be the heavens with black, yield day to night! Comets, importing change of times and states, Brandish your crystal tresses in the sky, And with them scourge the bad revolting stars That have consented unto Henry's death!

❀ MAJOR ❀ CHARACTERS

King Henry VI: Young and inexperienced; ascends the throne during a time of war with France and bickering amongst his noblemen.

Charles (Dauphin of France): Desperately trying to regain French territory captured by Henry V.

Richard Plantagenet/Duke of York: Discovers a family secret that will change the course of his life—and England.

Duke of Gloucester: Henry's uncle, who rules in his stead until he is old enough to take over.

Duke of Somerset: His conflict with the Duke of York eventually comes at a great cost for the English.

Lord Talbot: Fierce and heroic general of the English troops—greatly feared by the French.

THE STORY

The play opens at the funeral of King Henry V, who had been a very highly revered leader within England, successful against the French during the ongoing Hundred Years' War. Henry V's brothers—the Dukes of Bedford and Gloucester—and uncle—the Duke of Exeter—agree to form a regency council to rule during the tumultuous times, while the newly crowned Henry VI is prepped to take over.

Word comes that there is trouble in France. A rebellion—led by the French dauphin, Charles—is gaining momentum in regions acquired by Henry V, and England's fiercest warrior, Lord Talbot, has been captured during the Siege of Orléans. Bedford heads to France head the English troops.

Meanwhile, Charles is introduced to Joan la Pucelle (Joan of Arc), who claims to have had visions of how the French can defeat the English. A dubious Charles challenges her to a fencing match, which she promptly wins. Charles puts her in charge of the French army.

When Bedford arrives in France, he negotiates for Talbot's release. They attack and retake the city of Orléans while the French retreat.

Back in London, a quarrel between Richard Plantagenet and the Duke of Somerset is escalating. They each pick a rose—Plantagenet a white one and Somerset a red one—and ask each of their fellow noblemen to pick the same color rose as the man he supports. Plantagenet learns from his uncle, Mortimer—imprisoned in the Tower on London—that Plantagenet's father had been in line to the throne, but when he attempted to claim it, he was executed. Mortimer dies, and Plantagenet is motivated to restore his family's status and claim his birthright—the throne. Henry VI grants Plantagenet the titles of his deceased father and uncle, so he becomes the Duke of York.

Henry travels to France and, upon his arrival, is informed that Burgundy—a French leaderfighting with Talbot—has switched allegiances to Charles and the French. Talbot tells Henry that he will personally convince

Burgundy to change his mind.

When asked to choose sides between York and Somerset, Henry urges peace, absentmindedly picking up a red rose, unaware that his selection indicates an allegiance with Somerset. York says nothing.

Talbot runs into trouble and is trapped by French forces outside of Bordeaux. Henry orders York and Somerset to come to his aid, but their discord interferes with their duty. The English are defeated, and both Talbot and his young son are dead.

York and Somerset unite in battle against the French, capturing Joan of Arc and burning her at the stake. Meanwhile, Suffolk has captured a young, beautiful French noblewoman, Margaret. Suffolk plans to play matchmaker with the king and Margaret. If successful, Suffolk intends to use Margaret to influence to king.

Henry receives a letter from the Pope urging him to end the war and make peace with the French. Charles reluctantly agrees to the peace terms—which make him a viceroy under Henry's rule—though he secretly vows to eventually drive the English out of France.

Suffolk tells Henry about Margaret, and the young king is sufficiently intrigued to agree to marry her—despite being urged by Gloucester to marry a different woman.

Henry VI, Part 2

SUFFOLK:

As by your high imperial majesty
I had in charge at my depart
for France,
As procurator to
your excellence,
To marry Princess Margaret
for your grace,

MAJOR CHARACTERS

Henry VI, Duke of York, Duke of Gloucester, and Duke of Somerset **(see pages 44-45)**

Duke of Suffolk: Infatuated with Margaret, with the intention of satisfying his hunger for power through her.

Queen Margaret: Married to Henry but loyal to—and in love with—Suffolk.

Jack Cade: A commoner with a serious beef against literacy and a thirst for noble blood.

Lord Clifford: One of Henry's supporters who single-handedly quashes Cade's rebellion.

THE STORY

The play picks up where Part 1 left off (see page 51)—with the imminent marriage of Henry VI and Margaret. Suffolk has succeeded in his plan to manipulate Henry through Margaret, who is complicit with—and the probable lover of—Suffolk.

There are several conspiracies brewing in the court, each with intentions of getting certain players out of the way to ultimately attain either the throne itself or at least closer proximity to it. Beaufort (Cardinal of Winchester and great-uncle of Henry), the Duke of Buckingham, and the Duke of Somerset plan to oust Gloucester from his position as protector to the king. Meanwhile, the Earls of Salisbury and Warwick speak to York about wanting to squelch the influence of Suffolk and Beaufort. York sides with them, feeling it is not yet time to make his own attempt to attain the throne.

Gloucester's wife—who has her own designs on becoming queen—is arrested for dabbling in witchcraft when she hires a conjurer and a witch (who are complicit with Suffolk) to look into the future. She is banished, and Gloucester is shamed into giving up his position. Henry appoints Somerset as regent in France.

York seizes this opportunity to tell Salisbury and Warwick of his rightful claim to the throne. Both men swear allegiance to him. Suffolk accuses Gloucester of treason, having him arrested. Before he's able to proclaim his innocence at trial, Gloucester is murdered in his sleep. Suffolk is implicated in his death, and Henry banishes him from the country. On his voyage, Suffolk is murdered and beheaded by pirates.

Somerset returns with the news that France has been lost to the French. Word arrives of unrest in Ireland, and Henry gives York an army and sends him there to suppress the revolt. Before leaving, York hires Jack Cade to pose as the rightful heir in order to suss out how receptive the public would be to an attempt to take over the throne. Cade is successful in raising a significant and passionate army of commoners, and they kill many noblemen in their way to London, where Cade orders massive destruction and declares himself mayor. When Henry hears of the uprising, he leaves London for safety. Henry's supporter, Lord Clifford, eventually convinces Cade's army to give up the rebellion. Cade flees London and is killed a few days later when he is caught stealing from a garden.

York returns from Ireland, calling for Somerset's arrest for his duplicitous dealings regarding France. When Henry denies his request, York publically declares Henry as unfit to rule and announces his claim to the throne. A battle ensues at St. Albans, where York is joined by his sons, Edward and Richard. Somerset and Clifford are both killed, and York is ready to declare victory. But Henry,

Margaret, and Lord Clifford's son—who vows revenge for his father's death—have fled back to London.

ICONIC LINE

The first thing we do, let's kill all the lawyers.

—Dick the Butcher

Henry VI, Part 3

WARWICK:
I wonder how the king escaped our hands.

MAJOR CHARACTERS

Henry VI, Duke of York, Duke of Gloucester, and Duke of Somerset **(see pages 44-45)**

Queen Margaret **(see page 54)**

Edward York: Richard York's eldest son, who eventually takes over his father's struggle; becomes Edward IV.

Richard York: Richard York's son, born with physical deformities, secretly determined to attain the throne.

Clifford: Supporter of Henry and out

for revenge on York for having killed his father in the Battle of St. Albans (see page 60).

Earl of Warwick: Plays a pivotal role in getting Edward to the throne but switches sides after Edward makes a rash decision that has Warwick looking like a fool.

THE STORY

The play begins right after Part 2 left off (see page 60)—with York and his followers in the throne room of the palace. Just as York sits down on the throne, Henry and his followers enter. York makes his claim to the throne.

The weak leader that he is, Henry proposes a deal to York: that Henry be allowed to rule until his death, upon which the crown will pass to York and his descendants. York agrees and leaves. Henry's followers are shocked by his submission, and Margaret is so disgusted by his willingness to disinherit his own son, Prince Edward, that she leaves him.

Margaret has raised an army and launches an attack on York—the Battle of Wakefield. The Yorkists are defeated, and York's young son, Edmund, is killed by Clifford (revenge for York's killing of Clifford's father during the Battle of St. Albans).

Clifford and Margaret then capture York and torment York, eventually stabbing him to death.

Edward and Richard receive news of their father's death and are both devastated and determined to continue his fight. The tide turns at the Battle of Towton, with Edward's forces victorious. Clifford has been killed. Henry flees to Scotland and Margaret to France. Edward crowns himself Edward IV and gives titles to his brothers Richard and George. In an aside to the audience, Richard reveals his own ambitions to ascend the throne someday. Henry is captured and imprisoned in the Tower of London.

In France, Margaret appeals to King Louis XI for military aid in restoring Henry to the throne. Warwick has also traveled to France on behalf of Edward, proposing that Edward marry Louis's sister-in-law, thereby ensuring peace between the two countries going forward. News arrives, however, that Edward has rashly married a beautiful widow, Lady Grey (Elizabeth). Humiliated, Warwick switches allegiance over to Henry—even offering his daughter as a bride for Prince Edward—and leads French troops in battle against Edward. Edward IV's brother, George, is also disappointed in his marriage and abandons him to support Henry.

Edward VI is taken prisoner. Although Henry is restored as king, it is in name only—he appoints George and Warwick to rule as Lord Protectors. Edward is soon sprung from captivity by his followers, including his son Richard.

At the Battle of Barnet, George switches allegiances back to Edward. Warwick is killed, and Henry is once again captured and imprisoned in the Tower of London. The Yorkists are victorious in the Battle of Tewkesbury, and Edward subsequently kills Prince Edward and banishes Margaret to France. Edward's brother, Richard, goes to the Tower to kill Henry, who, before dying, prophesizes Richard as the cause of widespread destruction and suffering.

The play closes with much celebration surrounding the end of the war and birth of the king's son, also named Edward. No one suspects Richard's steely ambition to attain the throne himself (see page 67).

Henry VIII

PROLOGUE:

I come no more to make you laugh: things now,
That bear a weighty and a serious brow,
Sad, high, and working, full of state and woe,
Such noble scenes as draw the eye to flow,
We now present.

MAJOR CHARACTERS

King Henry VIII: He wants what he wants!

Cardinal Wolsey: Conniving, greedy, and duplicitous advisor to the king.

Anne Boelyn/Bullen: Expresses sympathy for Queen Katherine and says she would never want to be queen. Yeah right.

Queen Katherine: Henry's loyal and devout (Catholic) wife of nearly twenty years.

Thomas Cranmer, Archbishop of Canterbury: Religious advisor to the king, who has his back when it comes to malicious rumors.

THE STORY

The play opens with a group of three noblemen—the Duke of Buckingham, Duke of Norfolk, and Abergavenny—complaining about Cardinal Wolsey. The king's most trusted advisor, Wolsey is seen as power hungry, ruthless, and greedy, not only by the nobility, but also by the commoners, who are not happy about new taxes being levied on them. Buckingham has been arrested and charged with treason—a move that he is sure

Wolsey is behind.

Katherine speaks to the court on behalf of the king's subjects in opposition to the new taxes. Henry orders a stop to them. Wolsey secretly takes credit for being the one to repeal the taxes—an attempt to improve his reputation among the commoners.

For laughs, the king and a couple of his men disguise themselves as shepherds and crash a grand party at Wolsey's house. There, a beautiful young woman named Anne Boelyn captures his eye. Wolsey unmasks the king, who assures Anne that he will not forget about her.

Buckingham is found guilty of

treason and sentenced to execution. Word on the street is that Buckingham was set up by Wolsey—and rumors are also afloat that the king wishes to separate from Katherine. In fact, Henry has filed a divorce petition with the Pope. Katherine begs Henry to not divorce her and openly accuses Wolsey of being behind the whole thing. Though he appreciates Katherine's loyalty, the king still wants to pursue the divorce—whether or not he receives a green light from the Pope. He and Anne are quietly married.

Private letters between Wolsey and the Pope are intercepted by the king, who is infuriated to learn that Wolsey had secretly advised the Pope to wait to grant the divorce until Henry's infatuation with Anne has subsided. Henry strips Wolsey of his office and confiscates his property. Shortly after his arrest, Wolsey dies. Queen Katherine—demoted to a "Princess Dowager"—has grown tired and claims her death is at hand.

Free from the spell of Wolsey, Henry is troubled by new allegations of wrongdoing by his close advisor, Cramner, the Archbishop of Canterbury. Henry gives his ring to Cramner to "prove" his innocence at his trial, a move that signals to the trouble-stirring nobles that they've messed with the wrong man and that the infighting should stop.

Anne is crowned in a lavish coronation ceremony, and all marvel at her beauty and grace. The play concludes at the baptism of baby Elizabeth. Cramner speaks eloquently about her future greatness and all the good that she will bring to England.

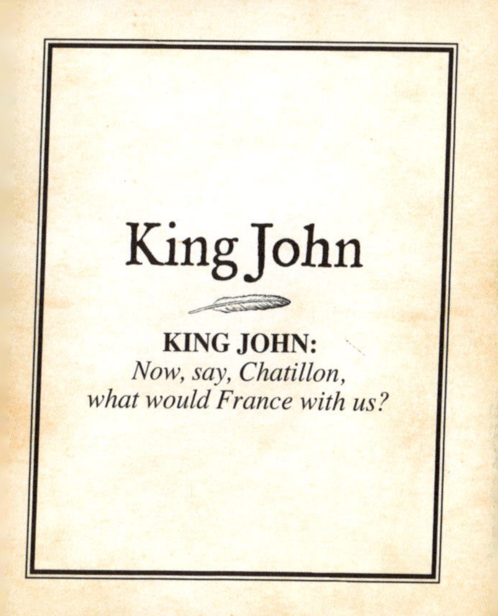

King John

KING JOHN:
Now, say, Chatillon,
what would France with us?

MAJOR CHARACTERS

King John: The legitimacy of his rule is called into question; he ends up alienating himself from the Pope and his own nobles.

Arthur: Son of John's older brother and therefore the rightful heir to the throne.

Philip "The Bastard": The illegitimate son of John's brother, Richard the Lionhearted; becomes one of the king's most fierce and dedicated supporters and warriors.

Philip, King of France: Wishy-washy instigator.

Cardinal Pandulph: Ambassador of the Pope; becomes the middleman in the strife between England and France.

THE STORY

As the play opens, King John receives a message from Philip, the king of France, who is demanding that John give up the throne to his nephew, Arthur, or else prepare to go to war. John, of course, refuses.

In the meantime, John is asked to settle a dispute between two brothers, the youngest of whom bears a strong resemblance to the king's late brother, King Richard I. The king's mother, Elinor, convinces the Bastard—as he is referred to—to give up the dispute with his brother and accept knighthood instead.

Philip and his forces take over the English town of Angiers. When King John and his forces arrive, they ask the townspeople who they think should rule over the town. They refuse to pick sides until the Bastard proposes that the French and English unite to conquer Angiers, at which point the townspeople suggest an alternative, which is that Philip's son, Louis, marry John's niece, Blanche, in order to achieve peace. Louis and Blanche are married.

Pandulph, an ambassador of the Pope, arrives with orders that John be excommunicated for having disobeyed the wishes of the Pope. Pandulph then commands Louis to overthrow John and forces Philip to join, despite the fact that John and Philip are now family.

War breaks out. The English forces capture Arthur, and John sends the Bastard back to England to seize the finances of the monasteries to fund the war. John puts his chamberlain, Hubert, in charge of Arthur and instructs him to kill him—in so many words. Hubert finds himself unable to kill Arthur and allows him to escape. Arthur dies from a fall. John's noblemen believe that he had Arthur killed, and therefore switch allegiance to Louis. John swears allegiance to the Pope and asks Pandulph to negotiate peace with the French on his behalf.

Meanwhile, the Bastard returns with English forces, and the fighting continues, with substantial casualties on both sides. Many of John's noblemen return to his side after learning that Louis plans to have them all executed once he wins the war.

John is poisoned by a monk and

dies. Just as the Bastard prepares for another attack on Louis, word arrives that Pandulph has negotiated peace with the French. The Bastard and noblemen all swear allegiance to John's son, who is to become Henry III.

Richard II

KING RICHARD II:

Old John of Gaunt, time-honour'd Lancaster, Hast thou, according to thy oath and band, Brought hither Henry Hereford thy bold son, Here to make good the boisterous late appeal, Which then our leisure would not let us hear, Against the Duke of Norfolk, Thomas Mowbray?

MAJOR CHARACTERS

King Richard II: Self-absorbed, oblivious, and doomed.

Henry Bolingbroke: Capable, convincing, and determined to take the throne from Richard.

THE STORY

The play opens in the court of Richard II—a stately but young king who spends excessive money on the latest fashions and his close friends; raises taxes to support frivolous wars; and is out of touch with his country's commoners.

Two noblemen, Henry Bolingbroke (son of the Duke of Lancaster and Richard's cousin) and Thomas Mowbray (the Duke of Norfolk) have brought a dispute to the king. Bolingbroke has accused Mowbray of misusing funds given to him by Richard for military purposes—and of the recent murder of the Duke of Gloucester (which was likely ordered by the king, himself).

With the quarrel unresolved, Bolingbroke and Mowbray challenge each other to a duel. Before the fight actually begins, though, Richard stops everything and declares that Bolingbroke is to be banished from

England for a period of six years and Mowbray for the rest of his life.

John of Gaunt (Duke of Lancaster and father of Bolingbroke) is so distraught over his son's exile that he dies. Richard seizes all of Lancaster's money and lands to fund a pet war in Ireland. Upon hearing the news of his disinheritance, Bolingbroke decides to assemble an army, return to England, and overthrow Richard—who has departed for Ireland. Bolingbroke is aided in his efforts by many noblemen, who are also disgruntled by Richard's poor governance decisions and selfish practices.

The turnover in power is relatively

peaceful, with no battle ensuing. Bolingbroke and his followers capture Richard in Wales and go back to London. Bolingbroke declares himself Henry IV and imprisons Richard in a remote area of north England. Newly crowned, Henry orders the execution of nearly all of Richard's supporters. The Duke of Aumerle (cousin to both Bolingbroke and Richard—though loyal to Richard) plots to poison Henry, but fails. Acting on a vague suggestion from the new king, Exton kills the imprisoned Richard. Henry publically denounces the murder, exiles Exton, and plans a trip to Jerusalem to cleanse himself of any "indirect" involvement he might have had in Richard's death.

ICONIC LINE

It is as hard to come
as for a camel
To thread the postern
of a small needle's eye.
—King Richard

Richard III

GLOUCESTER:
Now is the winter of our discontent
Made glorious summer
by this sun of York;
And all the clouds that
lour'd upon our house
In the deep bosom of the
ocean buried.

❁ MAJOR ❁ CHARACTERS

Richard, Duke of Gloucester: Shrewd, intelligent, and ruthless—one of the most power-hungry villains in all of Shakespeare's plays.

Duke of Buckingham: Richard's right-hand man in his rise to power.

Lady Anne Neville: Widow of Henry VI's son, Edward, who is somehow beguiled by Richard into marrying him.

Princes Edward and Richard: They see right through their uncle's schemes to get the throne—though this does not change their tragic fate.

❧ THE STORY ❧

After years of civil war between the Yorks and the Lancastrans, there is finally peace in England under the rule of Edward IV. Unfortunately, the king's younger brother, Richard is jealous and bitter (mostly because his physical deformity, which includes a hunchback) and greedy for the throne for himself.

Richard begins his ruthless campaign to get rid of everyone between him and the crown. First, he has his older brother, Clarence, imprisoned because of a prophecy implicating Clarence in the death of Edward's heirs. Next, he "woos" (with lies and false promises) a widow, Anne, and convinces her to marry him—after all, a king must have a queen. Little does Anne know that Richard is responsible for her husband's death, as well as her father-in-law (both Lancastrans).

Richard sends two men to the Tower of London to murder Clarence. The men tell Clarence that Richard sent them there to kill him, but Clarence doesn't believe them. Clarence is stabbed and then drowned. Richard manipulates Edward IV—

already very ill—into feeling guilty for Clarence's death, which advances his illness. Edward dies, leaving Richard as the Lord Protector until Edward's eldest son grows up.

Edward's two sons—Edward and Richard—are put in the Tower of London, and Richard has all of the princes' noble supporters executed. Richard continues—with his cousin, the Duke of Buckingham—his campaign as the rightful heir to the throne. He claims that the two princes are illegitimate and that he is merely a devout man with no aspirations to greatness. (Ha!)

Richard asks Buckingham to murder the two princes, but he refuses. So, Richard hires someone else to do the deed. When Richard also goes back on his word to give Buckingham new lands, Buckingham deserts Richard and sides with the exiled Henry, Earl of Richmond.

Richard decides a better wife for him would be Princess Elizabeth—the princes' sister (meaning she is Richard's niece). Richard poisons and kills Anne to get her out of the way. By this time, though, Queen Elizabeth (widow of Edward IV, mother of the two princes and Princess Elizabeth) is onto him and manages to stall him.

Henry, the Earl of Richmond, returns to England, bringing an army with him. The night before the big Battle at Bosworth Field, Richard is visited by the ghosts of his victims, who all wish death upon him. Richmond kills Richard in battle the next day. Richmond is crowned Henry VII and marries Princess Elizabeth.

ICONIC LINE

A horse! a horse! my kingdom for a horse!

—King Richard

PART II: TRAGEDIES

Antony AND Cleopatra

PHILO:

Nay, but this dotage of our general's O'erflows the measure: those his goodly eyes, That o'er the files and musters of the war Have glow'd like plated Mars, now bend, now turn, The office and devotion of their view Upon a tawny front: his captain's heart,

MAJOR CHARACTERS

Marc Antony: A shrewd and fearless leader who—like so many other men—turns to putty around Cleopatra.

Cleopatra: Gorgeous, theatrical, and volatile, she once also turned Julius Caesar to putty.

Octavius Caesar: Julius Caesar's adopted son, who is destined to become the first Roman Emperor; pragmatic and unemotional.

THE STORY

It is after the death of Julius Caesar (see page 133), and Marc Antony rules the Roman Empire along with Octavius Caesar and Lepidus. Antony is in charge of the easternmost section of the empire and is based in Alexandria, Egypt. Though he has a wife back in Rome, Antony carries on a passionate love affair with Egypt's queen Cleopatra, which distracts him from his civil duties.

The play opens with Antony receiving word from Rome that his wife has died and that Pompey seems to be preparing for rebellion against the triumvirate. Antony is summoned back to Rome. Cleopatra begs him not to go, but he repeatedly reassures her of his love and sets off.

Back in Rome, Antony marries Caesar's sister, Octavia, for political purposes—purely to solidify the triumvirate. Cleopatra flies into a rage of jealousy when she hears of Antony's marriage but is eventually calmed when she's reminded of her incomparable beauty and charms. She's certain Antony will return to her.

Antony, Caesar, and Lepidus negotiate a peace with Pompey. After Antony departs for Athens, Caesar breaks the truce with Pompey and defeats him. Caesar also accuses Lepidus of treason and imprisons him. Antony is infuriated by this news and returns to Alexandria (without Octavia), where he raises an army to fight Caesar.

Despite the superiority of Caesar's naval fleet, Antony decides to battle Caesar at sea. In the middle of the battle, Cleopatra's ships flee, and Antony follows, leading to his defeat. Antony forgives Cleopatra, of course, demanding merely a kiss from her to make up for his humiliating military failure.

Caesar writes to Cleopatra, asking her to betray Antony and come over to his side, which she seems to consider until Antony declares he will fight another battle in her honor.

The fight begins on land, but when Caesar switches to a sea battle, Cleopatra's ships flee once again. Antony is infuriated and resolves to kill Cleopatra, who thinks the best way to win his love back is by having word sent to him that she is dead. When Antony receives the news, he attempts to kill himself with his sword but manages to only wound himself. When he hears that she is alive, he manages to make it back to her before dying in her arms.

Caesar travels to Alexandria and tries to persuade Cleopatra to give herself up. Instead, she commits suicide with several poisonous asps. Caesar orders a military funeral for Antony and declares that Cleopatra be buried beside him.

Coriolanus

FIRST CITIZEN:
Before we proceed any further, hear me speak.

ALL:
Speak, speak.

FIRST CITIZEN:
You are all resolved rather to die than to famish?

MAJOR CHARACTERS

Caius Martius/Coriolanus: Roman general; honorable and a fantastic military leader, but also a bit of an elitist snob—and a mama's boy.

Tullus Aufidius: Military leader of the Volscians; very competitive—in a high school jock sort of way—with Martius.

Volumnia: Martius's mother; she has great influence over him.

THE STORY

As the play opens, there has been rioting in Rome, where the commoners—plebians—are angry at having been denied access to the city's supply of grain. The plebians are granted five representatives—called tribunes. One person unhappy with this decision is Caius Martius, a patrician general in the Roman army. He doesn't feel the plebians deserve such privileges because they do not serve in the military.

War breaks out with a neighboring group, the Volscians, who are led by Tullus Aufidius, the sworn enemy of

Martius, who is second in charge of the Roman army. The Romans win the battle that ensues, and the city of Corioles is taken, largely due to the heroics of Martius, who is given the name Coriolanus.

Coriolanus is urged by his mother, Volumnia, to run for a consul. He easily wins approval by the senate, but two plebians, Brutus and Sicinius, stir opposition to him amongst the commoners. Coriolanus is so infuriated that he lets loose a rant against the whole notion of popular rule. Brutus and Sicinius accuse Coriolanus of being a traitor, and he is exiled from Rome.

Out for revenge, Coriolanus approaches Aufidius, in Antium, and the two plan to attack Rome on a united front. Camped with Aufidius just outside of Rome, Coriolanus is visited by his mother, who begs him to call off the attack. Coriolanus is persuaded and, instead of fighting, brokers peace between the Volscians and Romans. Coriolanus and Aufidius return to Antium, where Coriolanus is heralded as a hero. Jealous, Aufidius accuses Coriolanus of treachery in going back on his word to capture Rome. A group of Aufidius supporters fights and kills Coriolanus.

Hamlet

BERNARDO:
Who's there?

FRANCISCO:
Nay, answer me: stand, and unfold yourself.

BERNARDO:
Long live the king!

MAJOR CHARACTERS

Hamlet: Danish prince who is full of conflict and contradiction; manages to be both thoughtful and rash.

Claudius: Ambitious, with a lust for power . . . and his dead brother's wife.

Gertrude: Hamlet's mother who, despite her love for her son, seems to have no problem with marrying her dead husband's brother.

Ophelia: Young and beautiful, she obeys her brother and father, but descends into madness.

THE STORY

The setting is Denmark. The king, Claudius, has recently ascended the throne after the death of his brother and has even married his brother's widow, Gertrude. Gertrude's son, Hamlet, is visited by the ghost of his father, who informs him that he was poisoned by Claudius. The ghost orders Hamlet to avenge his father's murder. Hamlet—unsure as to whether the ghost should be trusted—decides to look into the matter, putting on an act of madness as a distraction.

Polonius is one of Claudius's advisors, and also father to Ophelia and Laertes. Polonius suggests that Hamlet's erratic behavior might be due to his love for Ophelia—and advises his daughter to be wary of him.

A traveling troupe of actors visits, and Hamlet works with them to put on a play that tells the ghost's story—hoping to elicit some sort of telling response from Claudius. Sure enough, Claudius quickly and anxiously leaves the room during the murder scene—which Hamlet deems adequate proof of his guilt.

Hamlet angrily confronts his mother to determine whether she is complicit in his father's murder.

Polonius eavesdrops on their argument from behind a tapestry hung on the wall. Fearful that Hamlet may harm Gertrude, Polonius cries out. Hamlet stabs the tapestry and kills Polonius.

Claudius sends Hamlet away to England—secretly arranging for him to be killed on the way—but Hamlet manages to escape and return. Meanwhile, Ophelia goes mad after Polonius's death and drowns in a river. Laertes—goaded on by Claudius—blames Hamlet for the deaths of his father and sister. Claudius suggests a fencing match between Hamlet and Laertes. In order to ensure Hamlet's death, Laertes is going to dip his sword in poison, and Claudius plans to make sure Hamlet's drink is poisoned, as well.

At the match, Hamlet scores first but doesn't take a drink from his goblet. Instead, Gertrude proposes a toast with it, takes a drink, and dies. Laertes wounds Hamlet, who doesn't die immediately from the poison and manages to injure Laertes with his own sword. As he's dying, Laertes confirms that Claudius was responsible for the death of Hamlet's father. Hamlet stabs Claudius with the tainted sword and makes him drink the rest of the poisoned wine. Claudius dies, followed by Hamlet.

ICONIC LINE

The lady doth protest too much, methinks.
—Hamlet

Julius Caesar

FLAVIUS:
Hence! home, you idle creatures get you home:
Is this a holiday?

❦ MAJOR ❦ CHARACTERS

Julius Caesar: Roman senator and general; though not driven by ambition, he ignores several warnings of impending doom.

Marcus Brutus: Close friend of Caesar who puts his devotion to the republic above all else.

Caius Cassius: Mastermind of the plot against Caesar; motivated by jealousy and opportunity.

Marcus Antonius/Marc Antony: Close ally of Caesar with some ambition of his own (see also page 108).

THE STORY

The play opens in the streets of Rome, where a parade is being held in honor of Caesar's triumphant return from war. Two city leaders (tribunes)—Flavius and Murellus—chide the parade goers for neglecting their work. Caesar is warned to "beware the Ides of March" (March 15), but he pays no heed to it.

Two of Caesar's closest allies, Brutus and Cassius, discuss their concern over Caesar's growing popularity with the people, who, they fear, may want Caesar to be king—which would dispense with the republic. Cassius tells Brutus that they have themselves to blame for allowing Caesar to become so popular.

That night, Cassius hatches his plot to overthrow Caesar. In order to convince Brutus to join in, Cassius forges a bunch of letters from supposed citizens concerned about Caesar's growing power. The letters do the trick, and Brutus—ever loyal to fundamental tenants of the republic—agrees to the plan to lure Caesar from his house to kill him.

At the Senate one morning, the conspirators encircle Caesar and stab him one by one. When he sees his BFF, Brutus, joining in, Caesar poses his infamous question (which is actually rhetorical): "Et tu, Brute?" Caesar dies. Antony—who had purposefully been kept from the Senate—swears that his friend's death will be avenged.

Brutus gives a public speech, declaring his love for Caesar. He asserts, however, that Caesar had become too powerful for the good of the republic, for the liberty of its people, and that Caesar's only motivation was ambition. Antony arrives and reads Caesar's will, which bequeaths money to each citizen of Rome and declares that his private gardens become public. The crowd becomes enraged and drives Brutus and Cassius from the city.

Caesar's adopted son and appointed successor, Octavius, forms an alliance with Antony and Lepidus, and they prepare to battle Brutus and Cassius, who are raising an army outside the city. The ghost of Caesar visits Brutus—who is heavy with guilt—to say that they will meet again on the battlefield.

At one point during the battle, Cassius learns that his BFF, Titinius, has been killed. Distraught, Cassius asks one of his men to kill him. Turns out that Titinius is very much alive, but when he comes across Cassius' body, he is so upset that he kills himself. With the battle not going well and defeat imminent, Brutus impales himself on his own sword. The war over, Antony says that Brutus was honorable—truly acting in what he thought was in the best interest of the republic—and says that he will have a dignified burial.

ICONIC LINE

Friends, Romans, countrymen,
lend me your ears.
—Antony

King Lear

KENT:

I thought the king had more affected the Duke of Albany than Cornwall.

MAJOR CHARACTERS

King Lear: Wants the flattery and power of being king—even after giving up the position.

Cordelia: Honorable and loyal to her father—despite his rejection of her.

Edmund: Ambitious and seething with resentment at being the illegitimate son of an earl.

Edgar: Gloucester's legitimate son, who spends most of the play in disguise as several different characters.

Regan and Goneril: Lear's ruthless,

competitive, and utterly unscrupulous daughters.

Gloucester: Like Lear, he initially trusts the wrong child, which leads to his downfall.

THE STORY

King Lear, of England, wants to retire and plans to divide the country between his three daughters, Goneril, Regan, and Cordelia. He promises a larger area to the daughter who says she loves him the most. Goneril and Regan declare their immense love for their father, but Cordelia sincerely tells him that words cannot express her love. Feeling rejected (and totally missing her point), Lear disowns Cordelia and divides the country between his other two daughters. He also banishes the Duke of Kent for trying to defend Corelia. Despite Cordelia's lack of dowry, the King of France marries her, so she leaves to be with him.

Meanwhile, Edmund, the illegitimate son of the Earl of Gloucester, is determined to be recognized by his father and the court. He devises a plan to convince Gloucester that his legitimate son, Edgar, is plotting against him. At the same time, he tells Edgar that someone is plotting against him, so Edgar disguises himself as a beggar/madman named Tom.

Once they have power, Goneril and Regan both treat Lear with great disrespect. Disappointed by both of them, Lear starts to go mad. Kent returns to England disguised as Caius and becomes one of Lear's servants.

Disgusted by Lear's mistreatment by his daughters, Gloucester decides to intervene and sends a letter to the King of France asking for aid. The letter is intercepted, though, and Gloucester's eyes are gouged out. Regan turns him out to wander the heath, where he encounters his son,

Edgar, disguised as Tom, who tends to him.

Soon, Regan and Goneril—though both married—are competing for the affections of Edmund, involving him in various plots to get rid of their husbands and play a significant role in fending off the imminent French attack.

The French forces (and Cordelia) arrive, and a battle ensues. The English are victorious, and Edmund orders the execution of Lear and Cordelia.

The play concludes with lots of deaths. Edgar, now disguised as a knight, duels with Edmund and kills him, then takes off his disguise, the shock of which is at least partially responsible for Gloucester's death. Goneril poisons Regan and then stabs herself. It is too late for Cordelia, though—she is hanged. Lear dies of grief. Albany (Goneril's honorable husband) and Edgar assume power over the reeling country.

ICONIC LINE

Have more than thou showest,
Speak less than thou knowest.
—The Fool

Macbeth

FIRST WITCH:
When shall we three meet again
In thunder, lightning, or in rain?

SECOND WITCH:
When the hurlyburly's done,
When the battle's lost and won.

MAJOR CHARACTERS

Macbeth: A brave Scottish general filled with both ambition and self-doubt.

Lady Macbeth: Ruthless, power-starved, and portrayed as more masculine than her husband.

Banquo: A successful general, like Macbeth, who doesn't take the witches' prophecies to heart—unfortunately for him.

Macduff: Scottish nobleman whose fate is intertwined with Macbeth's.

❧ THE STORY ❧

As Macbeth and Banquo—two Scottish generals—return home after a successful war with Norway and Ireland, they encounter three witches who prophesy that Macbeth will become Thane of Cawdor and then King of Scotland, but also that Banquo's heirs will include a line of Scottish kings.

Macbeth receives word that the king has given him the title Thane of Cawdor as a reward for his valor in the war. This gets Macbeth wondering about the witches' other predictions, which he shares with his wife.

Macbeth and his wife conspire to murder the king, who will be visiting them at their castle, Inverness.

Macbeth ends up killing the king and his two guardsmen—whom he implicates in the king's murder. The king's two sons, Malcolm and Donalbain, flee the country, fearing their own lives are in danger. Macbeth is crowned king. Next up, Macbeth hires some men to kill Banquo and his son—Banquo is killed, but his son, Fleance, escapes. At a feast later that night, Banquo's ghost appears—but only to Macbeth, who appears to be going mad talking to it.

Fearful and desperate to know the future, Macbeth seeks out the witches and asks them to tell him what's going to happen. They tell him three things: one, he should beware Macduff; two, he cannot be harmed by anyone born of a woman; and three, he is not in danger until Birnam Wood comes to Dunsinane Castle.

Macduff has fled Scotland to join up with Malcolm, who is raising an army to overthrow Macbeth. Macbeth orders Macduff's castle to be stormed and his family to be killed—including his wife and young son. When he hears of this, Macduff swears revenge.

Meanwhile, Lady Macbeth descends into her own guilt-derived madness and eventually kills herself.

Macbeth fortifies himself in Dunsinane, feeling fairly secure—until, that is, he hears that the English army approaches, using branches cut from Birnam Wood to camouflage their advance, fulfilling part of the witches' prophecy. The battle begins, and Macbeth meets revenge-thirsty Macduff, who informs Macbeth that he was "from his mother's womb/ Untimely ripp'd." Maduff wasn't "born"—his mother had a cesarean delivery. The third part of the witches' prophecy comes true when Macduff slays and beheads Macbeth.

The battle ends, Malcolm is crowned, and peace returns to Scotland once more.

ICONIC LINE

Double, double toil and trouble;
Fire burn and cauldron bubble.
—Three witches

Othello

RODERIGO:
Tush! never tell me; I take it much unkindly
That thou, Iago, who hast had my purse
As if the strings were thine, shouldst know of this.

MAJOR CHARACTERS

Othello: The Moor—a much-respected and accomplished general in the Venetian military who's nursing some massive insecurities.

Desdemona: Othello's wife, a Venetian noblewoman.

Iago: Othello's ensign, who is out for revenge after having been passed over for a promotion; the ultimate Shakespearean villain.

Cassio: Young, handsome, charming, and recipient of the promotion Iago felt he deserved.

Emilia: Iago's wife (poor thing!) and attendant to Desdemona.

Roderigo: A wealthy but disgruntled former suitor of Desdemona; a pawn in Iago's plot to destroy Othello.

THE STORY

The play opens in Venice with an argument between Roderigo and Iago. Roderigo—a wealthy but foolish nobleman—had been paying Iago to help him win the hand of the beautiful Desdemona and is upset by the news of her marriage to Othello. Roderigo lashes out at Iago, who is, himself, seething with resentment for Othello, who had recently passed him over and promoted the younger, less-experienced Cassio to lieutenant. Iago convinces Roderigo to inform Desdemona's father that she has been "stolen" and beguiled into marriage by Othello's use of witchcraft.

Othello enters the scene and explains that it was his stories of travel and adventure that had won Desdemona over—not witchcraft—which Desdemona, herself, confirms. By the end of his defense, Othello has gained everyone's sympathies, though not without receiving a prediction—made by her own father—of Desdemona's betrayal.

News comes that the Turks are planning an invasion of Cyprus, so Othello (with Desdemona), Iago, and Cassio are all sent off to defend the island. Upon arrival on Cyprus, Othello is informed that the Turkish fleet has been destroyed in a storm. Othello calls for a feast to celebrate the averted war.

Iago starts feeding Othello's insecurities by suggesting that there might be something "inappropriate" going on between Desdemona and Cassio. At the same time, Iago convinces Roderigo to start a public brawl with Cassio in order to shame Cassio.

After his embarrassing fight with Roderigo, Cassio makes several attempts to make amends with Othello, including appealing to Desdemona for her help. After a series of unfortunate misunderstandings and with Iago's near-constant prodding, Othello is convinced that Cassio and Desdemona are having an affair and becomes consumed with jealousy. Iago promises Othello that he will murder the traitor Cassio.

Meanwhile, Iago convinces Roderigo that he must kill Cassio in order to get him out of the way on his path to Desdemona. In the confrontation, Cassio ends up stabbing

Roderigo. Iago comes onto the scene and wounds Cassio before killing Roderigo in apparent retribution for his attack on Cassio.

Othello approaches Desdemona as she sleeps and accuses her of infidelity. She awakens and proclaims her innocence. But to no avail—Othello will not be swayed, and he smothers her. Emilia and Iago enter and ask what has happened. When Othello tells them, Emilia realizes that Iago is behind everything. She clears up the misunderstandings that led to the perception that Desdemona and Cassio were having an affair. Othello begins weeping for his mistake, and

Iago flies into a rage and kills Emilia before trying to flee, unsuccessfully. Othello expresses his regret before killing himself with a sword. Iago is ordered to be executed.

ICONIC LINE

O! beware, my lord, of jealousy;
It is the green-ey'd monster
which doth mock
The meat it feeds on.
—Iago

Romeo AND Juliet

PROLOGUE:

Two households, both alike
in dignity,
In fair Verona, where
we lay our scene,
From ancient grudge break
to new mutiny,
Where civil blood makes
civil hands unclean.

MAJOR CHARACTERS

Romeo: Of the Montague family; sixteen years old, handsome and intelligent, though immature.

Juliet: Of the Capulet family; thirteen years old, beautiful and trusting, though very sheltered.

Friar Lawrence: A Franciscan friar sympathetic to the plight of the young lovers.

Mercutio: Romeo's BFF; witty, confident, and bawdy—the life of the party.

Paris: Juliet's Capulet-family-approved suitor.

Tybalt: Juliet's cousin, staunch defender of the Capulets.

THE STORY

In Verona, Italy, there is a feud raging between two noble families—the Montagues and the Capulets. Completely fed up, Prince Escalus, ruler of the city, has declared that the next person to instigate violence on behalf of the feud will be executed.

Enter Romeo, moping about—he is infatuated with a woman named Rosaline, but his feelings are unrequited. Romeo's friend, Mercutio, and cousin convince him to come along with them and crash a feast to be held at the Capulet's house that evening.

Meanwhile, Paris is asking Juliet's father for her hand in marriage. Her father agrees but asks that they wait two years, as Juliet is only thirteen years old.

At the feast, Romeo spots Juliet across the room and simultaneously falls in love with her and forgets about Rosaline. Romeo is recognized and a ruckus ensues as he, Mercutio, and his cousin are thrown out of the party. But not before he and Juliet lock eyes and have their first magical kiss.

When they learn of each other's identities, both are distraught. On his way off of the estate, Romeo passes by Juliet, ensconced on her balcony, and they express their love for one another.

Romeo confides in his friend, Friar Lawrence, who secretly marries the forbidden lovers the next day.

Tybalt, Juliet's cousin, challenges Romeo to a duel over his crashing of the feast. Romeo—now related to Tybalt through his secret marriage to Juliet—begs Tybalt to call off the duel. Mercutio offers to fight in Romeo's stead. Romeo inserts himself into the ensuing scuffle, but Tybalt stabs and kills Mercutio. Furious over his friend's murder, Romeo kills Tybalt and flees, now an outlaw.

Friar Lawrence devises a plan for Romeo to escape to Mantua—after spending his last night in Verona with his new bride. The next day, Juliet learns that her father has made plans for her to marry Paris in three days. Unsure of what to do, she seeks advice from Father Lawrence, who concocts a plan for her to join Romeo in Mantua. The friar gives Juliet a potion to take the night before her marriage to Paris. The potion will make her appear dead. When she is placed in the Capulet crypt, the friar will give her another potion to wake her up, and she will be free to join Romeo.

Romeo, now in Mantua, never receives the letter from the friar informing him of the plan. When he hears of Juliet's "death," he is despondent, returning to Verona to kill himself (by drinking poison) in Juliet's tomb. Juliet awakens from her fake death to see Romeo's body. She attempts to kill herself by kissing his poison-tainted lips. It doesn't work, so she stabs herself in the chest with a dagger.

Coming upon the lifeless young lovers, Montague and Capulet agree to end their feud.

ICONIC LINE

O Romeo, Romeo!
wherefore art thou Romeo?
—Juliet

Timon of Athens

POET:
Good day, sir.

PAINTER:
I am glad you're well.

POET:
I have not seen you long:
how goes the world?

PAINTER:
It wears, sir, as it grows.

MAJOR CHARACTERS

Timon: Wealthy and generous—and ripe for disillusionment.

Flavius: Timon's servant, who tries to warn him of his financial troubles but is ignored; he weeps at what becomes of Timon.

Apemantus: Poor and bitter from the start.

THE STORY

Timon is a wealthy and generous citizen of Athens who gives away his possessions and money to anyone who flatters him. He bails his friends out of jail and is a patron of any artist—poets, painters—who asks for his support. Timon derives pleasure from helping others and from their companionship.

Timon throws a feast, and a great crowd gathers—most of them wanting to get something from the host. Apemantus is the exception—he is a bit of a misanthrope and has come to snub his nose at the whole scene. Flavius, Timon's servant, seems to be the only one worried that Timon will, at some point, have given away everything and be left with nothing. Sure enough, that day comes, and

Timon's creditors start knocking at his door.

Timon asks his "friends" for help in paying his debts, but no one comes forward to assist him. Disgusted to realize that they had been so greedy and shallow and false, Timon invites everyone to another feast at his house. When everyone sits down to eat, the dishes are uncovered to reveal stones and water. He curses them all, denounces society, and leaves the city to live in a cave.

While foraging for food, Timon finds a hidden stash of gold. He buries all but a bit of it, which he keeps. Once word spreads of Timon's find, he starts getting visitors. Alcibiades—a disgruntled military leader—explains that he intends to raise an army to invade Athens, so Timon gives him most of the gold to further his purpose. Apemantus swings by to accuse Timon of copying his sarcastic and negative attitude.

Flavius seeks out Timon to give him the very last of his money. Timon realizes that Flavius was actually dedicated to him but laments the fact that Flavius is a servant. Two senators from Athens visit Timon and acknowldge that he had been badly treated, encouraging him to return to the city (and—more importantly—to convince Alcibiades to call of his attack). Timon curses them and sends them off.

Alcibiades is eventually placated by the senators and withdraws his forces. But then word comes that Timon has died alone in his cave, a misanthrope in the end.

Titus Andronicus

SATURNINUS:

Noble patricians, patrons of my right, Defend the justice of my cause with arms, And, countrymen, my loving followers, Plead my successive title with your swords: I am his first-born son, that was the last That wore the imperial diadem of Rome;

MAJOR CHARACTERS

Titus Andronicus: Honor and revenge are the two motivators of this tragic hero.

Tamora: Revenge is her motivation, and she seems to have no qualms about destroying innocent people in order to attain it.

Lavinia: Titus's only daughter; the victim in one of the most heinous crimes in all of Shakespeare's plays.

Aaron: There doesn't appear to be anything he wouldn't do for his lover, Tamora.

❧ THE STORY ❧

Titus Andronicus is an honorable Roman general returning home after ten years of war with the Goths. With him, he brings four of his twenty-five sons, as well as prisoners: Tamora (Queen of the Goths), her three sons, and Aaron, a Moor and Tamora's secret lover. According to custom, Titus sacrifices Tamora's oldest son in honor of his twenty-one sons who died in battle.

The Roman emperor has recently died, and Titus is encouraged to take over. He refuses, though, backing the emperor's oldest son, Saturnius—even offering his daughter, Lavinia, to him as a wife. Problem is that Lavinia has already been promised to (and is already in love with) Saturnius's brother, Bassianus. A hubbub ensues, and Saturnius ends up marrying Tamora, which puts her in the perfect position to exact revenge on Titus for her son's death. Aaron will be her means.

First, Aaron convinces Tamora's two living sons to murder Bassinius to get him out of the way so they can rape Lavinia. They do both, severing Lavinia's hands and tongue afterward to keep her silent. Aaron forges a letter that implicates Titus's sons, Martius and Quintus, in the death of Bassinius, so Saturnius sentences them both to death.

Aaron falsely tells Titus that Saturnius will pardon his sons if Titus cuts off his own hand and sends it to the emperor, which he does. Disgusted by the gesture, Saturnius returns Titus's hand to him, along with the heads of Martius and Quintus. Filled with rage and grief, Titus sends his son Lucius to partner with the Goths and plan to invade Rome.

Titus has begun to go mad, so Tamora and her sons disguise themselves as ghosts—Revenge, Rape, and Murder—and tell Titus that he will get revenge on all of those who have wronged him, as long as he tells Lucius to call off the attack. Titus tells Lucius to prepare a feast to celebrate peace. Tamora leaves, and Titus kills her sons.

At the feast the next day, Titus—believing it the honorable thing to do—kills Lavinia (her crime: allowing herself to be raped). Titus also informs Tamora that her sons are dead and have been baked into the pie she's been eating. Titus kills Tamora; Saturnius kills Titus; and then Saturnius is killed by Lucius. In the end, Lucius is crowned emperor. Saturnius is to be given a proper burial, while Tamora's body will be fed to wild animals, and Aaron is buried up to his chest and left to die of thirst/starvation. Phew!

PART III: COMEDIES

All's Well That Ends Well

COUNTESS:
In delivering my son from me,
I bury a second husband.

MAJOR CHARACTERS

Helena: Beautiful orphan determined to get her man, even if he doesn't seem like that great of a catch to the rest of us.

Bertram, Count of Rousillon: Handsome but an utter cad.

Diana: The virginal object of Bertram's affections.

THE STORY

Helena is a young, beautiful orphan of a famous physician and the ward of the Countess of Rousillon. Helena is in love with the countess's son, Bertram, but, in spite of her beauty, Bertram doesn't give her the time of day.

The King of France has taken ill, and Helena goes to Paris to treat him, using techniques and knowledge learned from her father. She is successful in treating the king's condition, and, in thanks, the king offers her marriage to any man she wishes. Helena chooses Bertram, who is horrified but, of course, goes through with the marriage.

Shortly afterward—and before the marriage is consummated—Bertram leaves for Venice. He sends a letter to Helena saying that she will never truly be his wife until two conditions are met: one, she wears his family ring; and two, she is pregnant with his child. He says neither will ever happen. Distraught, Helena decides to take a religious pilgrimage.

Meanwhile, in Venice, Bertram is trying to seduce a young virginal woman, Diana. Helena ends up in Venice and overhears Diana and her mother discussing Bertram's advances. Helena ends up staying with Diana and her mother and pays them to go along with a scheme to get her husband back.

First, Diana is to pretend to return Bertram's affections. They exchange rings as tokens of love (Diana passes Bertram's ring on to Helena), and Bertram finally weasels his way into her bed . . . or so he thinks. Helena is actually in the bed when the count climbs in. The final part of Helena's plan involves messengers arriving in Venice to announce Helena's "death."

Upon hearing the news of his wife's death, Bertram returns home to Rousillon, followed by—unbeknownst to him—Diana, her mother, and a very much alive Helena. There, while everyone mourns Helena's death, Diana, her mother, and Helena enter, and Helena declares that Bertram's two conditions have been met! Bertram promises to be a good husband to her, and there is merriment—though whether the ending is truly happy has been debated over the centuries since the play was written.

As You Like It

ORLANDO:

As I remember, Adam, it was upon this fashion bequeathed me by will but poor a thousand crowns, and, as thou sayest, charged my brother, on his blessing, to breed me well: and there begins my sadness.

MAJOR CHARACTERS

Orlando: Handsome, kind, and thoughtful.

Rosalind/Ganymede: Adventurous, charming, and very clever.

Celia/Aliena: Devoted, loving, and sweet.

Oliver: Starts out as a self-serving and neglective of his younger brother, Orlando, but has a life-changing experience in the forest.

Duke Frederick: Starts out as cruel and power hungry, but does a 180 before the end of the play.

Duke Senior: Placid and even-tempered, the rightful ruler of the dukedom.

THE STORY

Oliver and Orlando are brothers whose father has just died. Oliver inherits all of his father's estate and refuses to take care of Orlando.

Meanwhile, Duke Frederick has usurped and exiled his older brother, Duke Senior, who sets up a simple camp in the Ardenne forest. Frederick has allowed Duke Senior's daughter, Rosalind, to stay behind, as she is the BFF of Frederick's daughter, Celia.

Rosalind and Orlando see each other one day and fall in love at first sight. After it becomes clear that his brother will not look after him, Orlando decides to leave—with his father's former page, Adam—also for the Ardenne forest. Duke Frederick has changed his mind about Rosalind, banishing her from court. She and Celia disguise themselves—Rosalind as the young man, Ganymede, and Celia as a shepherdess, Aliena—and flee to the forest, as well. When he hears of his daughter's disappearance—which coincides with Orlando's disappearance—Duke Frederick forces Oliver to lead the search party, threatening to take away his lands if everyone is not found.

In the forest, Orlando finds refuge with Duke Senior, who lives a simple but satisfying life with a group of lords who left court voluntarily after he was exiled. Rosalind/Ganymede and Celia/Aliena purchase a cottage in the woods and befriend a shepherd, Silvius, who pines for a shepherdess named Phoebe. Rosalind, dressed as Ganymede, runs into Orlando, who explains how he is lovesick for a woman named Rosalind.

Meanwhile, Phoebe falls in love with Ganymede/Rosalind, cruelly rejecting Silvius. Oliver and Celia, dressed as Aliena, also fall instantly in love and decide to marry. Rosalind decides it's time to put an end to the disguises. The play ends with the gigantic wedding—officiated by Hymen, the god of marriage—of Oliver and Celia, Rosalind and Orlando, Silvius and Phoebe, and Touchstone (Celia and Rosalind's chaperone in the forest) and Audrey (a country girl). Frederick has a change of heart and returns the throne to Duke Senior.

ICONIC LINE

All the world's a stage,
And all the men and
women merely players.
—Jaques

THE Comedy OF Errors

AEGEON:

Proceed, Solinus,
to procure my fall
And by the doom of death
end woes and all.

MAJOR CHARACTERS

Egeon: In search of his son, Antipholus of Syracuse.

Antipholus of Syracuse: In search of his long-lost mother and twin brother, Antipholus of Ephesus.

Antipholus of Ephesus: A successful, married merchant, who is apparently not in search of anyone.

THE STORY

Egeon, a merchant from Syracuse, has been arrested—and sentenced to execution!—in the city of Ephesus for breaking a law that prevents people from traveling between the two cities. In a desperate attempt for leniency, he tells his story.

Many years before, he had a wife and twin sons, who had twin slaves. There was a shipwreck, and he saved one son (Antipholus of Syracuse) and slave (Dromio), while his wife and the other son and slave were washed away and never to be seen again. Just recently, Antipholus had set out with his slave to try and find his mother and brother. The duke grants Egeon a day to come up with the money to pay his fine, or else be executed.

Little does Egeon know that Antipholus and Dromio are also in Ephesus, in disguise. And little do they all know that Egeon's lost son is a well-respected citizen of Ephesus, where he lives with his wife and slave. Naturally, with two twin men and two twin slaves running around the city, much confusion and many amusing scenarios unfold—including accusations of theft and madness.

The whole thing is finally pieced together by an abbess, Emilia, who turns out to be Egeon's long-lost wife and mother of the twins. The whole family is reunited, and the charges against Egeon are dropped.

Cymbeline

FIRST GENTLEMAN:

You do not meet a man but frowns:
our bloods
No more obey the heavens
than our courtiers
Still seem as does the king.

❦ MAJOR ❦ CHARACTERS

Cymbeline: A wise and merciful leader who is, unfortunately, under the influence of his conniving new wife.

Imogen: Cymbeline's daughter; beautiful, resourceful, and devoted.

Iachimo: Clever but scheming Italian who doesn't appear to have much respect for women.

Posthumus: A little too quick to turn on his wife, don't you think?

THE STORY

As the play opens, Cymbeline, the British King, is furious to learn that his daughter, Imogen, has secretly married a poor gentleman named Posthumus. With his plans to marry Imogen to his new, oafish stepson Cloten ruined, Cymbeline exiles Posthumus to Italy.

While in Italy, Posthumus meets an Italian rouge named Iachimo and tells him all about his love for Imogen. Iachimo claims that all women are, at base, unfaithful, and bets Posthumus that he can return to England and seduce Imogen. Of course, Imogen rejects Iachimo's advances, so he hides in a chest that he has delivered to her room, where he steals a bracelet that Posthumus had given to her. When Posthumus sees the bracelet, he becomes enraged at Imogen's apparent infidelity that he sends a servant, Pisanio, to kill her. Pisanio doesn't believe Iachimo's claim, though, and advises Imogen to disguise herself as a boy and travel to Italy to clear things up with Posthumus. In the meantime, Pisanio reports back to Posthumus that he did indeed kill Imogen.

Imogen loses her way in Wales and encounters an exiled nobleman, Belarius, and his two "sons"—who are, in fact (though unbeknownst to them) the sons of Cymbeline, whom Belarius had kidnapped in retaliation to his having been exiled.

Cloten arrives in search of Imogen and ends up fighting with one of the sons, who kills and beheads him. Imogen feels ill and drinks a potion that her stepmother had given her. The queen had meant for the potion to be a lethal poison, but, in fact, it makes Imogen only appear to be dead. When she wakes next to Cloten's beheaded body, she thinks he is Posthumus.

Meanwhile, a Roman army is invading Britain. Posthumus and Iachimo travel with them, though

Posthumus actually fights on behalf of the British. Belarius and his "sons" join Posthumus in battle, and the Roman are defeated, upon which Posthumus disguises himself as a Roman prisoner—he has a death wish, believing that Pisanio had actually killed Imogen.

In the end, Imogen and Posthumus are reunited; Iachimo's treachery is forgiven; Cymbeline is reunited with his long-lost sons; Belarius is forgiven, as well; and Cymbeline even frees the Roman prisoners.

Love's Labour's Lost

FERDINAND:
Let fame, that all hunt
after in their lives,
Live register'd upon
our brazen tombs
And then grace us in the disgrace
of death;

❁ MAJOR ❁ CHARACTERS

Ferdinand, King of Navarre: A devoted scholar . . . and lover of women.

Princess of France: Up for a game of wits.

Berowne, Longaville, and Dumaine: Ferdinand's lords and fellow scholars.

Rosaline, Maria, and Katherine: Ladies in waiting of the princess, who are flirty and fun.

THE STORY

The play opens with Ferdinand, the King of Navarre, and his noblemen taking an oath to dedicate the next three years to scholarly pursuits and fasting. The oath specifically prohibits them from seeking the company of women. Berowne, one of the king's courtiers, reminds Ferdinand that they are expecting a visit from the Princess of France.

When the princess arrives, she is not allowed to enter the court, so she and her entourage are forced to camp out in a field.

There is a comical scene involving the king and his lords and the discovery that they have each fallen in love—instantly—with the princess and her ladies. They decide to visit the princess's camp in disguise, where the princess and her ladies are also in disguise. Once the disguises come off, they all sit down to enjoy a comic play.

At the end of the play, word reaches the princess that her father has died and that she must return home to take the crown. Ferdinand and his lords promise to be faithful to their women, who in turn tell them that they will have to prove their faithfulness by waiting to pursue them for a year and a day. The women decamp, and the play ends.

Measure for Measure

DUKE VINCENTIO:
Escalus.

ESCALUS:
My lord.

DUKE VINCENTIO:
Of government the properties to unfold,
Would seem in me to affect speech and discourse;

MAJOR CHARACTERS

The Duke: Spends most of the play disguised as a friar; a just and kind ruler.

Angelo: The hypocrisy of this politician is utterly timeless.

Isabella: On her way to becoming a nun when she is called to get her brother out of his predicament.

THE STORY

The setting is Vienna, where the Duke has decided to take a break from his duties, leaving the city for a while.

He puts Angelo in charge while he's away, along with Escalus, a trusted lord.

Angelo is very righteous and strives to clean up the immoral activity that seems to be taking over the city. Enter Claudio, who has gotten his fiancée, Juliet, pregnant before they are married. Angelo has Claudio arrested and sentences him to death. Upon hearing that her brother (Claudio) is going to be executed, Isabella—a novice nun who hasn't yet taken her vows—pleads with Angelo to spare her brother's life. Angelo offers to pardon Claudio on the condition that she give her virginity to him. Isabella says no—despite her brother's pleadings.

It turns out that the Duke had never left Vienna—instead disguising himself as a friar and observing Angelo's rule. The friar befriends Isabella and lays out a two-part plan to deal save Claudio and put Angelo in his place.

The first part of the plan involves Mariana, Angelo's onetime fiancée, whom he had rejected when her dowry was lost at sea. Isabella pretends to concede to Angelo's request—on the condition that they meet in absolute darkness and silence. Of course,

Mariana is the one who really sleeps with Angelo.

Of course, after doing to deed with "Isabella" (really Mariana), Angelo goes back on his word and gives Claudio's execution the go-ahead. The Duke/friar intervenes and makes sure that the head of another prisoner who's just died is sent to Angelo.

The Duke "returns" to Vienna, cause for great celebration. Isabella (believing her brother is dead) and Mariana make their accusations against Angelo, and he, of course, denies them. The Duke reveals that he was in disguise as the friar. He pardons Claudio and orders the execution of Angelo—only after he marries Mariana so that she may inherit his state. In the end, the Duke proposes to Isabella. She actually gives no answer—her response a mystery that's been debated over for centuries.

ICONIC LINE

What's mine is yours, and what is yours is mine.
—Duke

THE Merchant OF Venice

ANTONIO:

In sooth, I know not why I am so sad: It wearies me; you say it wearies you; But how I caught it, found it, or came by it, What stuff 'tis made of, whereof it is born, I am to learn;

MAJOR CHARACTERS

Antonio: Wealthy Venetian nobleman, sometimes interpreted as being in love with Bassanio.

Bassanio: Though he's squandered his estate, he's sincere in his love for Portia and his friendship with Antonio.

Shylock: A multidimensional bad guy; yes, he wants a literal pound of flesh, but he's also the victim of his circumstances—being Jewish in a Christian society that treats him poorly.

Portia: Beautiful, quick-witted, and resourceful—the typical Shakespearean heroine.

THE STORY

Bassanio is a young Venetian noble running short on cash but wanting to woo a wealthy heiress, Portia. He asks his friend, Antonio, to loan him the money. Antonio is generous and very wealthy, but his funds are presently tied up at sea. So, he promises to act as guarantor on a loan if Bassanio can find someone to loan him the money.

A Jewish moneylender named Shylock agrees to loan the money

to Bassanio, but with the stipulation that if it's not repaid on time, Shylock will be owed a pound of Antonio's flesh. Shylock despises Antonio, who's antisemitic and has badmouthed Shylock around town for charging huge interest rates on his loans. Antonio agrees to the loan.

Portia has many suitors, and her father's will stipulates that each of them must choose between three caskets—one of gold, one of silver, and one of lead. The one who chooses the correct casket (the one with her portrait inside) wins Portia's hand. Portia and Bassanio are already smitten with each other from a previous meeting, so she is happy to see him arrive to take the test. Bassanio picks the lead casket—the correct one. He and Portia are married.

Meanwhile, Shylock is infuriated to learn that his daughter, Jessica, has eloped with Lorenzo, who is Antonio's friend and a Christian.

Word arrives that Antonio's ships have wrecked. His creditors are knocking, so Bassanio heads back to Venice with money from Portia to repay Shylock. Portia and her maid follow, disguised as men—Portia as a lawyer. The due date for Bassanio's loan from Shylock's has passed, and Shylock wants his pound of flesh from

Antonio. He even refuses Bassanio's offer of three times the money that he is owed.

Portia—disguised as a lawyer—intervenes and points out a couple of flaws in Shylock's claim, and the tables are turned. In the end, Shylock's life is spared, but he is forced to convert to Christianity and leave all of his property and wealth to Jessica and Lorenzo upon his death.

The play ends with Portia informing Bassanio that she was actually the lawyer in disguise at the trial and with celebration of their good fortune and news that some of

Antonio's ships have returned safely after all.

ICONIC LINE

All that glisters is not gold.
—Prince of Morocco

THE Merry Wives OF Windsor

SHALLOW:

Sir Hugh, persuade me not;
I will make a Star-chamber matter
of it: if he were twenty Sir John
Falstaffs, he shall not abuse
Robert Shallow, esquire.

MAJOR CHARACTERS

Falstaff: Technically a knight, but old, overweight, wholly unclever, and quite a scoundrel.

Mistress Page/Mistress Ford: These country housewives were probably cackling over their pranks on Falstaff for decades afterward.

Anne Page: Turns out the joke is on her parents.

THE STORY

The central character of this play is John Falstaff, also from Henry IV (see page 20)—though this play takes place a couple of years later). Falstaff is running low on funds so decides to court a couple of married women—Mistress Ford and Mistress Page—to see if he can get money from them. He sends them each love letters, which turn out to be identical. The women decide to have some fun at Falstaff's expense.

Meanwhile, Page's daughter, Anne, is being courted by three different men. Her mother wants her to marry a French doctor, Caius; her father would like for her to marry a man named Master Slender; and Anne herself is in love with Master Fenton.

Hilarity ensues with a foiled duel; the Mistresses duping Falstaff into thinking they might actually respond to his advances; Falstaff hiding in a dirty laundry basket and being dumped in the river; and Falstaff in drag and roughed up.

Eventually, the wives come clean with their husbands regarding the fun they've been having with Falstaff. The four of them devise one last scheme, telling Falstaff to meet them in Windsor forest, where they arrange for several local children dressed up as fairies to ghosts to circle and terrify him. Finally, the Mistresses and their husbands emerge and explain the joke.

But where is Anne, neglected during all of the hubbub? She enters with Fenton, whom she has just married. The Page's give in and approve of the marriage, and everyone is off to celebrate.

ICONIC LINE

This is the short and the long of it.
—Mistress Quickly

A Midsummer Night's Dream

THESEUS:

Now, fair Hippolyta, our nuptial hour Draws on apace; four happy days bring in Another moon: but, O, methinks, how slow This old moon wanes!

❦ MAJOR ❦ CHARACTERS

Hermia/Lysander/Demetrius/ Helena: Young Athenians caught up in affairs of the heart.

Oberon/Titania: King and queen of the fairies who prove that even marriages between fairies contain rough spots.

Puck: Oberon's jester whose antics and mistakes drive the twists and turns—and laughs—of the play.

THE STORY

The play opens on the eve of the marriage of Theseus—Duke of Athens—and Hippolyta—Queen of the Amazons. Egeus, a nobleman, comes to complain to Theseus that his daughter, Hermia, is refusing to marry the man he has chosen for her, Demetrius. Instead, she is in love with Lysander. Theseus tells Hermia that she must marry Demetrius or be sent to a nunnery or perhaps even be executed. He gives her until his wedding to decide.

Hermia and Lysander plan to run away and be married. Helena—

Hermia's friend and in love with Demetrius, herself—tells Demetrius of their plans. The next night, Hermia and Lysander depart on foot through the woods, followed by Demetrius, followed by Helena.

In the woods, the king and queen of the fairies—Oberon and Titania—are squabbling over a young Indian prince given to Titania. Oberon overhears Demetrius and Titania arguing and enlists his jester, Puck, to seek out a flower whose juice makes a waking person fall in love with the first person her or she sees upon waking. Puck accidentally puts the juice on Lysander, who is awoken by Helena and instantly falls in love with her, rejecting Hermia. Oh boy. The four argue, with Demetrius and Lysander agreeing to a duel to prove which one loves Helena more. Oberon, enraged at Puck's incompetence, orders him to make sure the duel never happens. Puck mimics their voices so that they all become separated and lost in the woods.

Meanwhile—elsewhere in the woods—a group of men are rehearsing for a play they're planning to put on for the wedding. One man named Bottom sees Puck, so Puck turns his head into that of a donkey. Unaware of his transformation, Bottom sings to himself. His voice awakens a sleeping Titania, who instantly falls in love with him. Oberon uses this opportunity to take the Indian prince before releasing Titania and Lysander (and Bottom) from their spells. Demetrius is put under a spell, however, so that he falls in love with Helena.

There is a triple wedding: Theseus and Hippolyta, Lysander and Hermia, and Demetrius and Helena. The play Bottom and his fellow performers put on is so bad that it becomes a comedy. That night, the fairies enter the house and bless the sleeping newlyweds. Puck has the last lines of the play, telling the audience that perhaps even the play itself has been a dream.

ICONIC LINE

Lord, what fools these mortals be!

—Puck

Much Ado About Nothing

LEONATO:
I learn in this letter that Don Peter of Aragon comes this night to Messina.

MAJOR CHARACTERS

Claudio: Young soldier with come serious communication issues.

Benedick: As soon as he swears he will never marry, you know what's coming.

Beatrice: Clever and witty and even a bit of a feminist.

Hero: The typical Shakespearean heroine—beautiful, sweet, and the victim of a misunderstanding.

THE STORY

The play opens in the idyllic town of Messina, nestled in the Italian countryside. The governor, Leonato, has just received word that Don Pedro, a prince from Aragon, will be passing through on his way home from a recently won war. Don Pedro—and his party, which includes friends Claudio and Benedick, and his illegitimate brother, Don John—plan on staying in Messina for a month.

When the visitors arrive, Claudio quickly falls in love with Hero, Leonato's daughter, and they decide to marry. Benedick—a sarcastic confirmed bachelor—matches wits with Beatrice, Leonarto's niece, who is equally clever and intelligent. The others entertain themselves by playing a trick on Benedick and Beatrice—leading each to think the other is in love with him or her. Despite their cynical observations on love, each privately expresses openness regarding the notion of being together.

Don John decides to be a wet blanket on everyone's happiness by wooing Hero's maid one night in the darkness. Don Pedro and Claudio witness this but think that Hero is the one being wooed, not her maid. At the wedding, Claudio rejects Hero in front of everyone, accusing her of infidelity. She faints from shock, and her family members decide it best to pretend she has died until they can clear her name. Eventually the truth comes out, and Hero's innocence is proven—but Claudio believes she is dead.

Leonato demands that Claudio tell everyone in the town of Hero's innocence. Claudio must also marry Leonato's "niece," who is waiting for him in the church. When Claudio arrives at the church, he is amazed to see that the niece is actually Hero. He is overcome with relief and joy.

Everyone prepares for the double wedding of Claudio and Hero and Benedick and Beatrice.

ICONIC LINE

How much better is it to weep at joy than to joy at weeping!
—Leonato

Pericles, Prince of Tyre

PROLOGUE:

To sing a song that old was sung,
From ashes ancient Gower is come;
Assuming man's infirmities,
To glad your ear, and please your eyes.

MAJOR CHARACTERS

Pericles: Seems to be under the impression that the only way to get a wife is by winning a competition.

Thaisa: Lucky for her she actually falls in love with the man who wins her.

Dionyza: Wait to see what this mama bear will do for her cub.

Marina: Manages to beguile men by not sleeping with them.

THE STORY

Pericles, the Prince of Tyre, has traveled to Antioch to try to win the hand of King Antiochus's daughter. All Pericles has to do is answer a riddle. He figures it out but doesn't actually say the answer because the answer would reveal that Antiochus is having an incestuous relationship with his daughter. Sure that Antiochus is going to have him killed for finding out, Pericles flees and decides to travel for a while.

Pericles goes to Tarsus to visit king Cleon and his wife Dionyza, bringing them corn to help fight the famine that has beset their country. On the way home, Pericles's ship sinks, and he ends up in Pentapolis. He hears of a jousting contest the next day—the winner gets the hand of king Simonedes's daughter, Thaisa. Of course, Pericles wins, and Thaisa is very happy to marry him.

Pericles hears word that Antiochus and his daughter have died, so he decides to return to Pyre. On the way, Thaisa gives birth to a daughter, Marina, and appears to have died. She is put in a wooden coffin and set overboard. She ends up washing ashore Ephesus, where she is revived and—believing Pericles to have perished at sea—becomes a priestess in the temple of Diana. Heartbroken, Pericles decides to leave his newborn daughter to be raised by Cleon and Dionyza.

Sixteen years pass. Marina has grown to be very beautiful. Dionyza is annoyed because Marina is getting more attention from suitors than her own daughter, so she arranges for Marina to be killed. Before she's killed, Marina is captured by pirates, who sell her to a brothel in Myteline. Marina manages to hold onto her virtue and ends up working as a girls' teacher.

Pericles decides to return to Tarsus to get Marina, but is informed on his arrival that she has died. Distraught, he decides to travel. Naturally, he ends up in Myteline and is reunited with Marina. Diana appears to him in a dream and tells him to go to her temple in Ephesus. Pericles takes Marina along, and there they meet Thaisa—and the family is complete again.

Taming OF THE Shrew

SLY:
I'll pheeze you, in faith.

HOSTESS:
A pair of stocks, you rogue!

SLY:
Ye are a baggage: the Slys are no rogues; look in the chronicles; we came in with Richard Conqueror. Therefore paucas pallabris; let the world slide: sessa!

MAJOR CHARACTERS

Katharina: Her ill temper at the beginning of the play may be due to her father's favoritism of her younger, more beautiful sister.

Petruchio: Greedy, materialistic, and a chauvinist; but is there love beneath his treatment of Katharina?

Lucento: The opposite of Petrichio, his view of love is melodramatic and consuming.

Bianca: The opposite of her sister, Katharina, she is sweet and soft-spoken.

THE STORY

First off, the main part of a play is actually a play within a play, being performed as part of a joke on Christopher Sly, a poor, drunk tinker.

The play within the play takes place in Padua, Italy, where Lucentio has just arrived, with a couple of servants—Tranio and Biodello—to study at the university. He is quickly distracted by a beautiful and wealthy young woman he falls instantly in love with, Bianca. There are a few obstacles in Lucentio's way of having her, though. One, she has a couple of suitors already—Gremio and Hortensio—and, two, her father forbids her to be married before her outspoken and abrasive older sister, Katharina, is married, herself.

Lucentio decides to disguise himself as a Latin tutor to spend time with Bianca, while Tranio pretends he is Lucentio and befriends Bianca's father, Baptista.

Lucentio is in luck regarding his second obstacle. His friend, Petruchio, breezes into town openly declaring his only desire when it comes to marriage is that the woman be wealthy. Lucentio tells him about Katharina, and Petruchio is sold.

Petruchio is late to his own wedding and forces Katharina to go home with him immediately afterward, claiming that she must do whatever she says because she is now his property. There, he "tames" her by denying her food and sleep for days—all in the name of love and by using reverse psychology with excuses like, "This food isn't good enough for you, so you shall not have any." Eventually, Katharina will agree to anything her husband says, including when he calls the sun the moon.

Meanwhile, back in Padua, Bianca has fallen in love with her Latin tutor—Lucentio in disguise. Tranio—as Lucentio—offers Baptista a huge amount of money for Bianca's hand. Baptista says he must meet Lucentio's father so that he can verify that the money is real. Lucentio hires someone to pretend to be his father, Vincentio. Only problem is that the real Vincentio has come to town to visit his son. No matter, though—Lucentio and Bianca have eloped. When they return married, everyone's true identity is revealed.

Having lost Bianca to Lucentio, Hortensio marries a widow. At the celebration, everyone notices the drastic change in Katharina and congratulate Petruchio. Katharina gives a speech on the duties of a good wife. In the end, everyone is content, even Katharina.

THE

Tempest

MASTER:
Boatswain!

BOARSWAIN:
Here, master: what cheer?

MASTER:
Good, speak to the mariners: fall to't, yarely, or we run ourselves aground: bestir, bestir.

MAJOR CHARACTERS

Prospero: Forever in the pursuit of knowledge, he and his magic are behind all of the events of the play.

Miranda: Not too surprising that she falls in love with the first man—aside from her father—she ever encounters.

Ariel: A playful and mischievous spirit who can mimic voices, control the weather, and change shapes.

Caliban: Native to the island; likens himself to Prospero in that Prospero was usurped from his position as duke, just as Caliban was usurped of his on the island upon Prospero's arrival.

❧ THE STORY ❧

The play opens aboard a ship being tossed about in a tempest. Aboard are Alonso (King of Naples), Antonio (Duke of Milan), Ferdinand (Alonso's son), Gonzalo (a nobleman from Milan), Sebastian (Alonso's brother), Trinculo (a jester), and Stephano (a butler).

From the shore of a nearby island, Prospero and his daughter, Miranda, see the ship in distress. Prospero tells Miranda—for the first time—the story of how they came to be on the island. Twelve years before, Prospero had been the Duke of Milan. His brother, Antonio, had plotted to take his place and ordered a nobleman named Gonzalo to cast Prospero and Miranda to sea on a small boat. Without Antonio's knowledge, Gonzalo stocked the boat with food and water, and a whole bunch of books from his library. Prospero has spent his years on the island studying these books, which are all about magic and divination. The only other inhabitants of the island are a native, Caliban, and Ariel, a spirit—both servants to Prospero.

The ship sinks, but all of those aboard make it safely to the island. Ferdinand—separated from his shipmates and alone—happens upon Miranda. They fall in love at first sight—apparently the work of Prospero's magic. Miranda eventually ends up asking Ferdinand to marry her. Meanwhile, the others from the ship have landed on another part of the island, fearing Ferdinand to be dead. They set off in search of him. Alonso and Sebastian contemplate killing Antonio and Gonzalo while they sleep.

Trinculo and Stephano fall in with Caliban. They all get drunk, and Caliban devises a plot to kill Prospero, take Miranda, and make Stephano king of the island. They are distracted from their plot by Ariel's music, coming from another part of the island.

In the end, all convene in front of Prospero, who scolds but eventually forgives everyone—including his brother—for the harm they've either done to him or were planning to do to him. Prospero plans to resume his role as Duke of Milan, so everyone prepares to depart the island. But first, he frees Caliban and Ariel—but only after asking Ariel to ensure them a smooth voyage home.

ICONIC LINE

O, wonder!
How many goodly creatures
are there here! How beauteous
mankind is! O brave new world,
That has such people in't!
—Miranda

Troilus
AND
Cressida

TROILUS:

Call here my varlet; I'll unarm again: Why should I war without the walls of Troy, That find such cruel battle here within? Each Trojan that is master of his heart, Let him to field; Troilus, alas! hath none.

MAJOR CHARACTERS

Troilus: Trojan prince about to learn that love stories don't always have happy endings.

Cressida: Ulysses refuses to kiss her cheek because he can tell, just by looking at her, that she gets around.

Hector: Trojan prince—a great warrior, beloved by the Trojans.

Achilles: The greatest warrior of the Greeks, who is also a prideful brat.

THE STORY

It is year seven of the Trojan war, between the Trojans and the Greeks. Within Troy, Troilus—a young prince—complains of not being able to concentrate on the war, distracted by his love for Cressida, a fellow Trojan whose father has defected to the Greek side. He enlists the aid of her uncle, Pandarus, to get Cressida's attention.

In the Greek camp, general Agamemnon wonders why his men are acting so down and defeated. Ulysses places the blame on Achilles, who is setting a bad example by refusing to fight and spending all of his time alone with his lover Patroclus.

The Trojans have proposed a one-on-one battle between Prince Hector and one of the Greek warriors of their own choosing. Instead of choosing Achilles (the better warrior), Ulysses suggests nominating Ajax—a move intended to make Achilles angry and rejoin the fight to prove himself.

In Troy, there is some discussion as to whether Helen should be returned to the Greeks—whether she is worth all of the fighting. Hector is eventually convinced to continue with the war. Pandarus works it so that Cressida and Troilus have a few moments alone together, during which they declare their love for one another, and after which they consummate their love.

Cressida's father arranges for her to be traded with a Trojan prisoner so that she may join him in the Greek camp. Upon parting, the weeping lovers swear to remain true to one another.

Time for the fight between Hector and Ajax, which ends in a draw. Afterward, Achilles tells Hector that he will see—and kill—him on the battlefield the next day. In the meantime, there is a feast to celebrate the fight.

Troilus wants to find Cressida, and Ulysses agrees to take him to see her. They spy on her giving in to the advances of Diomedes, and Troilus is heartbroken and devastated. He swears that he will track down Diomedes on the battlefield the next day and kill him.

At first, the Trojans seem to be winning, but eventually, Achilles joins the battle and comes upon Prince Hector in an unguarded moment. Achilles and some others kill Hector, parading his body around the outskirts of Troy. At the end of the play, the Trojans are retreating, mourning their prince, while Trolius also mourns the loss of his Cressida.

Twelfth Night

DUKE ORSINO:

If music be the food of love,
play on;
Give me excess of it,
that, surfeiting,
The appetite may sicken,
and so die.

MAJOR CHARACTERS

Duke Orsino: Has a penchant for melodrama—his infatuation with Lady Olivia may be the classic case of a man wanting what he cannot have.

Lady Olivia: Also has a penchant for melodrama—but has some guts for marrying a man whom she thinks is merely a messenger.

Viola/Cesario: Resourceful and beautiful—a classic Shakespearean heroine.

THE STORY

Duke Orsino of Illyria is wallowing in his unrequited love of the beautiful Lady Olivia, who is mourning the recent deaths of her father and brother, and has sworn off all men for a period of seven years.

There is a shipwreck off the coast, and a young woman, Viola, washes ashore, assuming her twin brother, Sebastian, also on the ship, has drowned. Viola disguises herself as a man, Cesario, and goes to work in the household of Duke Orsino, who uses her as a messenger in his attempts to woo Olivia. Problem is that Viola has instantly fallen in love with Orsino, while Olivia quickly falls for Cesario, not knowing that he is really Viola in disguise. And there you have a perfect example of a love triangle.

Meanwhile, in Olivia's household, everyone is sick and tired of the puritan negativity of her steward, Malvolio, so they decide to play a trick on him, convincing him that Olivia, herself, has romantic designs on him. The whole rouse culminates in a hilarious scene in which Malvolio wears yellow stockings, crossed garters, and a permanent smile on his face while in the presence of Olivia—who believes that her steward's strange behavior is due to madness and has him locked away.

Sebastian survived the shipwreck, of course, and comes to Illyria, where he is mistaken for Cesario—even by Olivia, who asks him to marry her. Sebastian is confused because he has never met her before, but because she is beautiful and obviously wealthy, he goes along with it.

Orsino and Cesario go to visit Olivia, who greets Cesario (Viola) as her husband. Sebastian enters the room; Viola sheds her disguise; and the truth is revealed. In the end, Malvolio is released; and Duke Orsino asks Viola to marry him.

ICONIC LINE

Be not afraid of greatness:
some are born great, some achieve
greatness, and some have greatness
thrust upon them.
—Malvolio

Two Gentlemen of Verona

VALENTINE:
Cease to persuade,
my loving Proteus:
Home-keeping youth have ever
homely wits.

MAJOR CHARACTERS

Valentine: Starts the play making fun of Proteus for choosing love over travel and adventure.

Silvia: So gorgeous and charming that her father keeps her locked up in a tower at nights.

Proteus: He may be a gentleman, per the title, but he certainly doesn't act like one for most of the play.

Julia: Can you imagine having the man you love ask you to deliver the ring you gave to him to another woman?

❧ THE STORY ❧

The play opens with BFFs Valentine and Proteus saying farewell to each other. Valentine is heading off to do some traveling, while Proteus is staying behind in Verona because he cannot bear the thought of parting from the woman he loves, Julia. At first, Julia pretends not to be interested in Proteus. But when Proteus learns that his father is sending him to Milan, Julia realizes her love for him. They exchange rings and promises of their love before Proteus departs.

In Milan, Proteus finds Valentine, who's fallen in love with the Duke's daughter, Silvia—and she with him. Only problem is that the Duke wants Silvia to marry Thurio. Factor in Proteus also falling in love with Silvia at first sight, and you've got a real mess.

Valentine confides in Proteus his plan to elope with Silvia, and Proteus passes it along to the duke, who is outraged and banishes Valentine from the city. Julia gets wind of Proteus's affection for Silvia and travels to Milan disguised as Sebastian, a page boy, to see what's going on for herself. Proteus gives Sebastian the very ring that Julia had given to him, instructing the page to deliver it to Silvia. Julia is somewhat relieved to learn that Silvia rejects Proteus's advances, disgusted that he could so easily forget about the love that he left in Verona.

Meanwhile, Valentine is captured by a bunch of outlaws—like him, banished gentlemen—and they make him their leader. A rumor swirls around Milan that Valentine is dead, but Silvia won't believe it and sets out to find him. Proteus and Sebastian/Julia follow. At one point, Proteus rescues Silvia from the outlaws and, after she rejects him again, he kind of loses his cool and seems close to raping her. Valentine, who'd been secretly observing them, comes forward. Proteus apologizes for his behavior, and Valentine forgives him. Julia (as Sebastian) faints in all of the hubbub, and her identity is revealed—upon which Proteus instantly remembers his deep love for her and promises fidelity to her anew.

In the end, the two couples are married, and the Duke welcomes all of the outlaws back to Milan.

THE
TWO
NOBLE
KINSMEN:
Preſented at the Blackfriers
by the Kings Maieſties ſervants,
with great applauſe:

Written by the memorable Worthies
of their time;
{Mr. *John Fletcher*, and} Gent.
{Mr. *William Shakſpeare*.}

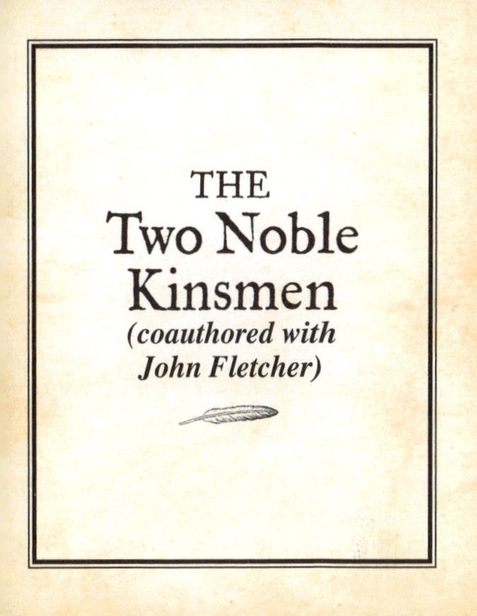

THE Two Noble Kinsmen

(coauthored with John Fletcher)

PROLOGUE:

New plays and maidenheads
are near akin—
Much follow'd both, for both
much money gi'n,
If they stand sound and well;
and a good play
(Whose modest scenes blush
on his marriage-day,
And shake to lose his honor)
is like her
That after holy tie and first night's stir,
Yet still is modesty, and still retains
More of the maid to sight than
husband's pains.

MAJOR CHARACTERS

Theseus and Hippolyta: The Duke of Athens and his wife.

Palamon and Arcite: Cousins and BFFs . . . who highly value honor and family.

THE STORY

The play is based on "The Knight's Tale" from Chaucer's *Canterbury Tales*. Theseus, Duke of Athens, has waged war on the tyrant, Creon of Thebes. Despite their disapproval, Palamon and Arcite—who are cousins/

kinsmen—fight on Creon's side and are taken prisoner in Athens. Through their prison window, they spy the beautiful Emilia, sister to Theseus's wife, Hippolyta. They begin to bicker over which one will have her.

Arcite is freed. Because he has been banished from Athens, he disguises himself as a peasant so as to not have to leave Emilia. Palamon, still in jail, catches the eye of the jailer's daughter, who helps him escape. He is still obsessed with Emilia, though, so he ignores her—even though she follows him. Wandering the woods, he encounters Arcite, who nurses the weary Palamon back to health. At the same time, they renew their bickering over Emilia and decide to duel for her.

Theseus comes upon them the eve of their duel and demands they be arrested and executed. They explain how they are motivated by their love for Emilia. Hippolyta and Emilia beg Theseus to reconsider, and so he gives them a month to prepare for a public contest of strength. The winner will get to marry Emilia. The loser will be executed. Meanwhile, the jailer's daughter is slowly restored to health by a doctor who suggests her fiancé pretend to be Palamon.

The day of the contest arrives.

Arcite wins but is soon after injured from being thrown from a horse. Luckily it is before Palamon's execution. On his deathbed, Arcite reconciles with Palamon and gives his blessing for him to marry Emilia.

THE Winter's Tale

ARCHIDAMUS:

If you shall chance, Camillo, to visit Bohemia, on the like occasion whereon my services are now on foot, you shall see, as I have said, great difference betwixt our Bohemia and your Sicilia.

MAJOR CHARACTERS

King Leontes: Proof that jealousy never leads to any good.

King Polixenes: Should he stay or should he go?

Hermione: So beautiful and charming that her husband is quick to suspect her of infidelity.

Perdita: Kind of like a female Oedipus, though this is a comedy, not a tragedy.

Florizel: His heart knows no socioeconomic boundaries.

THE STORY

At the beginning of the play, we are introduced to longtime friends King Leontes of Sicilia and King Polixenes of Bohemia. Polixenes has been visiting Leontes and is eager to return home to see his young son. Leontes, however, tries to convince him to stay longer. Unsuccessful, Leontes asks his wife, Hermione, to convince Polixenes to hang around longer. Polixenes decides to stay—which arouses suspicion in Leontes that perhaps his friend and wife have been having an affair and that the child his wife is carrying isn't really his. He asks Camillo, a nobleman, to poison Polixenes. Instead, Camillo tells Polixenes of Leontes's plan, and the two men flee.

Leontes accuses Hermione of infidelity and has her thrown in prison, while he waits to hear back from an oracle as to whether the child is his. Hermione gives birth to a daughter prematurely, and Leontes orders that the child be abandoned in a remote area. After this is done, word comes from the oracle exonerating Hermione and Polixenes. It is too late, though. Word comes from the prison that Hermione has died, and the child, named Perdita by Hermione, is lost.

Perdita is raised by a kind shepherd on the Bohemian coast. Sixteen years later, Florizel—the son of Polixenes—has fallen in love with Perdita. Polixenes intervenes, however, objecting over his son's lowly choice of a wife. Florizel and Perdita run away to Sicily, where they end up in the court of Leontes, who is still in mourning. Shortly afterward, Polixenes shows up, and it is eventually deduced that Perdita is Leontes's lost child. Leontes and Polixenes join in their approval of the young couple. Suddenly, a statue of Hermione appears to come to life. In fact, it is the real Hermione, who had gone to live in seclusion after losing her child. Hermione and Leontes are joyously reunited.

Credits

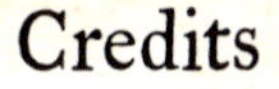

Illustration by Christopher Wormell: cover and p. 1

By permission of the Folger Shakespeare Library: pp. 18, 26, 34, 42, 52, 62, 72, 80, 88, 96, 106, 114, 128, 152, 172, 180, 188, 206, 212, 220, 226, 242, 264, 272, 288, 304, 312, 322

© Image Asset Management Ltd./ SuperStock: pp. 16, 136

Mary Evans Picture Library/Everett Collection: pp. 104, 120, 144, 162, 190, 234, 248, 280

© Stock Montage/SuperStock: p. 256

© Universal Images Group/SuperStock: pp. 198, 296